GO! GO! CHICHICO!

GERALDINE McCAUGHREAN

Illustrated by
TOM PERCIVAL

Barrington Stoke

First published in 2013 in Great Britain by
Barrington Stoke Ltd
18 Walker Street, Edinburgh, EH3 7LP

www.barringtonstoke.co.uk

This edition first published 2019

First published in a different form in *Football Fever*,
edited by Tony Bradman, published by Corgi, 1998

4u2read edition based on *Go! Go! Chichico!*
published by Barrington Stoke in 2013

Text © 2013 Geraldine McCaughrean
Illustrations © 2013 Tom Percival

A CIP catalogue record for this book is available
from the British Library upon request

ISBN: 978-1-78112-863-3

Printed in China by Leo

For Enzo

CONTENTS

Chapter 1 1

Chapter 2 7

Chapter 3 11

Chapter 4 16

Chapter 5 23

Chapter 6 28

Chapter 7 36

Chapter 8 41

Chapter 9 47

CHAPTER 1

Chichico was first down on the beach that morning.

A few gulls were pecking at the litter along the water-line, but no one else was about.

The sun was still so low that it bobbed like a big football on the sea. Chichico wanted to swim out and bring that football back to shore – then he would not have to wait for the others.

Chichico was always first down on the beach, but he could not start to play till Anna and Davi arrived with the ball.

They used their T-shirts for goalposts, and Anna and Davi both played against Chichico, because he was so good. As the morning wore on, more and more children arrived and joined in.

Sometimes rich boys from the big hotels along the back of the beach wanted to play. If Anna liked the look of them, she would point at their fancy trainers and say:

"Shoes off! Shoes off! No one here wears shoes!"

So the boys joined in with bare feet, and Chichico ran rings round them, while his friends sang:

"Go! Go! Chichico!"

The truth was that none of the local children had so much as one pair of shoes between them. But what did they care? The sand was soft.

That morning, two men stood at one of the hotel windows and watched the game on the beach below.

"Look how he wrong-foots them! Every time! Look at the speed of him!" one of the men said.

"And do you see how he controls the ball?" said the other. "Will I go down and have a word?"

"Yes, do that, will you?" the first man said. "And don't take 'no' for an answer."

CHAPTER 2

Chichico saw a man in a suit wave to him from the steps of the hotel. He tried not to look. The man was a stranger, and strangers never had anything good to say to a boy with no shoes. Last month a football had broken one of the hotel windows. This man was probably the manager of the hotel. He would want to make the children move the game on down the beach. But the man went on waving, and at last Chichico hopped and strolled over to hear what the man had to say.

"You ever heard of Santos?" asked the man in the suit.

"Santos who?" said Chichico. "I had an uncle Santos once …"

The man shook his head. "The football team, boy. Santos Brazil."

"I'd have to be dead not to have heard of them," said Chichico. "They're only the best team in the entire universe."

"Well, the Santos scout has been watching you," said the man. "Why not come for a trial on Friday? We might be able to make a real footballer of you. What's your name?"

Just for a moment, Chichico could not remember his name. He could not remember his name, or how to breathe, or even how to speak.

"Chi … Chi … Chi …" he said.

"OK, Chi Chi," said the man. "Be at the ground early on Friday. And remember to bring your boots."

CHAPTER 3

Chichico sat down on the hotel steps. They seemed to tip and roll under him like a raft at sea. Anna and Davi ran over.

"Are we playing football or what?" said Davi.

"Tell me I'm awake," said Chichico. "Tell me I'm not in a dream."

"I don't think so," said Davi, and he pinched himself.

"I've got a trial for Santos," Chichico told him. "On Friday."

Davi pinched himself again. "I think you must be dreaming after all!" he joked. "But I've got an idea – don't wake up till Saturday!"

"There's just one problem," said Chichico. "I need boots. I must have boots."

Davi waved his hand in the air like that was no problem at all. "Don't worry about that!" he said. "I'll buy you a pair. You can pay me back when you're a famous football star."

"You're the best, Davi," Chichico said, and raced away to tell his mother. His bare heels threw the sand up in clouds of golden dust.

Anna turned to Davi. "And just how are you going to buy a pair of football boots?" she asked. "Do you have any idea how much they cost?"

"I'll think of something," said Davi, who did not want his sister to spoil the happy mood. "Just so long as Chichico plays in those trials. That's what matters."

CHAPTER 4

On Friday, Anna went with Chichico to the huge white football ground on the hill. The ground was part of their lives – they all dreamed of a fairy tale in which they got to play there. Dozens of other boys were standing about, their legs shaking in terror, just like Chichico.

Davi was late.

"He's not coming, is he?" Chichico asked Anna. "He hasn't got the boots, has he? He just can't face telling me."

Anna was always loyal to her brother.
"He'll be here," she said. And she was right –
just then, there Davi was.

"Did you get them?" Chichico asked. "Did you? You did, didn't you?"

"Don't work up a sweat before you have to!" said Davi. He puffed out his chest and produced, like magic, the most amazing pair of shiny black football boots from behind his back. They had yellow diamonds on the sides, and laces like trickles of golden honey.

"They're only the best money can buy, that's all!" Davi crowed.

Before Chichico had time to thank him, a man came and pinned a number to the back of his vest.

Chichico opened his mouth to say something to Davi, but he could not find the right words.

"Get out on the pitch with the rest!" the man barked. Chichico did as he was told.

Anna turned to Davi with a frown. "All right," she said. "Own up. Where did you get them? Did you sell something? Our mother?"

"I just borrowed them," Davi said. "From the lockers in the changing rooms. They've probably played in cup finals, those boots!"

Davi tried to sound proud of himself, but he had never stolen anything before, and Anna could see he was scared right down to the soles of his bare feet.

"If you borrow something, you have to ask first," she said.

"There wasn't anyone ..."

"So write a note."

Davi looked surprised. "Do you mean I should confess?"

Anna shook her head. "No – an I.O.U. A note to say that you borrowed them. You could say it was an emergency."

"I can't spell 'emergency'," Davi said. He didn't even want to think about all the other words he couldn't spell.

"I'll write the note for you," Anna said, and hooked her arm under his to cheer him up. "We don't need to put your name on it. We'll slip it under the locker-room door. They'll understand. And after the trials I'll come with you to give them back. You can't get arrested for borrowing something. I'm sure of that. Almost sure."

Davi smiled. "I thought you'd be angry. Mum would be. Mum would say I was a sinner who will never get into Heaven."

"I don't think we need to tell Mum," said Anna. "Let's just make sure Chichico plays in these trials. One worry at a time."

CHAPTER 5

It was odd playing in boots. When Chichico set off to run, his feet felt like lead. He got to the ball, but even a tiny kick sent it high into the sky, over the line and into the empty seats.

"You're rubbish," said a boy in snow-white boots. He kicked Chichico's shin.

And his legs got so tired! He clumped about the grass like a little girl in her mother's high heels. Before long he was too slow even to stay in the game.

The ball came flying past him one last time, and he turned to play it. But the studs on the boots gripped the grass, and Chichico only fell over, hurting his knee.

"Who asked you to come?" jeered the boy in white boots.

A whistle blew.

"Take a break," called the coach. "Numbers 36, 7 and 20 can go home. We don't need you."

Chichico didn't need to check the number on his vest, but he did it anyway. 20. He had just thrown away the chance of his life.

He looked round him at the huge stands gleaming in the sun. Only once in his life had he ever had a ticket to see Santos play here. He remembered every minute – the flags, the drums, the whistles, the huge roar as Santos scored. Now the stands looked like a big white ship, sailing off without him.

CHAPTER 6

Chichico had to be rid of the football boots. Everyone's eyes were on the trials. It was easy for Chichico to creep into the dark building to hide them.

He said sorry to the boots. In his head, he said sorry to Davi for all the effort he had gone to.

But I can't play in boots, he thought as he stuffed them into the very back of a tin cupboard. *Of course I can't. I've never played in boots!*

Just then, a noise came from the door – a tiny scraping sound, so that Chichico froze in terror. Someone was going to come in. They would ask him what he was doing there – he would have to tell them ...

But the person at the door did not come in. A light pair of feet – or maybe two pairs – ran softly away down the long hall outside. Chichico waited five minutes, then his bare feet ran the same way. At the end of the tunnel, he bumped into Anna and Davi. They looked even worse than he had felt five minutes ago.

But then they had had to watch while Chichico let his big chance slip away from him for ever.

Anna smiled a kind smile. "What happened out there? Were you nervous? Was that it?"

Chichico grinned. "No! It was the boots! I can't play in boots! But it'll be all right now – the boots have gone. I got rid of them. Next

time I'll play in my bare feet – and then see! Can't stop now!" He hopped off along the stand, as light as a mountain goat on his bare brown feet.

Davi groaned from the bottom of his soul. "So he's got rid of the boots," he said. "Now I can't put them back. And I just wrote that note to say I took them! I'll go to prison, Anna! Then I'll go to Hell for stealing. I wouldn't have minded ... much, if Chichico had just got to play for Santos!"

Then Davi put his face in his hands and began to cry. Anna put her hand on his hair. "Don't worry," she said. "I'll come to prison with you. If they let girls in."

Out by the pitch the coach, too, groaned.

"No," he said to himself. "Nothing here. Not one spark of real talent."

"Excuse me, sir," said Chichico.

"Don't bother me, boy," the coach said. "You're number 20, aren't you? Go home. No second chances. We can't use you."

"Please, sir," said Chichico. "I can't go home."

"Scram."

"I can't go home, because someone has stolen my boots. If I go home without them, my wicked father will beat me and my poor mother will break her heart. And then what will become of my 15 brothers and sisters?"

The coach blinked at this story. "Boots?" he said. "I can't worry about boots now. Hang about till the trials are over and I'll send for the police."

"Yes, sir. Thank you, sir," said Chichico, and went and sat on a bench. After a moment, he stood up and said, "Maybe I could just go and kick the ball about while I wait."

"What?" the man asked. "In your bare feet?"

"Why not?" said Chichico. And before anyone could stop him, he had run onto the pitch.

CHAPTER 7

Chichico took the ball from the boy in white boots and snaked round two other players. Like a flash he had passed it to the wing, and as it came back to him he headed it into the top corner of the net.

In the box in the stand, the coach got to his feet.

After that, the other side seemed never to have the ball at all.

It spun between their legs, looped over their heads, vanished from the toes of their boots. And every time, Chichico smacked it into the goal.

In the stand, the coach stood on his seat to get a better view.

The boy in white boots tried to stamp on Chichico's bare toes, but the ref spotted him and sent him off. Before the boy got to the stand, Chichico had scored another goal.

The coach jumped up and down so hard that his seat broke.

"Sign that boy!" he shouted. "Sign the boy with the bare feet!"

"Now I can go to prison happy!" said Davi. "I think I'll go and tell them what I did."

"I'll go with you," said Anna, always loyal.

CHAPTER 8

The Santos first team were in the changing room, putting on their kit. Davi and Anna watched from the door, sure that someone was about to discover the robbery. Big beads of sweat broke out on Davi's brow. Anna saw them as she looked at him, and tears came to her own eyes to think she had helped to get this brother she loved so much sent to prison. Write a note! What ever had made her give him such stupid advice ...

Then she saw it. A midfielder's big foot was standing right on top of the note they had pushed in under the door. He had not seen it yet. No one had seen it. Now if Anna could only get it back ...

"What are you kids doing here?" the midfielder asked as he spotted Anna and Davi hanging about the door.

"I'm sorry ... Er ... We ... I mean ..." Davi said.

"We just wanted to get you to sign our vests," said Anna. She took a few steps into the room.

"Do you make a habit of going into men's changing rooms, little girl?" the midfielder asked in a cross voice. He was just about to push her out the door when he spotted the note under his foot. "What's this?"

A shout like a moose call boomed from the other side of the room. It was the Santos goalkeeper, who had his head inside a tin locker. "Eh! Enrico!" he shouted. "What are your boots doing in my locker?"

"Search me," said the player called Enrico. He took the black boots from the goalkeeper and started to put them on. Davi and Anna stared.

The boots were black, with diamonds of yellow and laces like trickles of golden honey. So that was where Chichico had "got rid" of them!

The midfielder opened the note and was just about to read it when Anna pulled it out of his hand.

"That's mine!" she said, and darted for the door, dragging Davi with her. Her voice came back along the hall behind her.

"It was just a fan letter, mister!"

Outside in the sun, Davi pulled away and leaned against a wall to get his breath back. He was panting and giggling all at once.

"Do me a favour, Anna," he said.

"What's that, Dav?"

"Let's not tell Chichico about any of this. It could spoil his focus."

"Do me a favour, Dav," Anna said instead of an answer.

"What's that, Anna?"

"Let's not tell Mum any of this. Ever!"

CHAPTER 9

The papers were full of it. Chichico was the youngest player from Brazil ever to play for the Santos first team.

And of course he was the first ever to play in a cup final with bare feet!

On the day of the game, his parents, his brothers and all his mates from the beach had tickets Chichico had got for them with his own wages.

They were up there now in the stand, waving flags, whistling and singing. And what did they sing? "Go! Go! Chichico! Go! Go! Chichico!"

Anna said to Davi at the half-time break, "He looks so tiny beside all those great big men."

"Don't be silly," said Davi. "It's not size or muscles that make a great footballer." Davi often said this. He was only knee-high to a grass-hopper himself.

In the second half, Chichico pelted up and down the pitch. He tackled, he passed, he headed the ball across the front of the goal and he marked a player two times as big as he was. It was an even, hard match. The crowd were holding their breath – they even stopped shouting near the end, for the first time anyone could remember.

It was then that Chichico heard a Santos player shout his name. He saw the ball at his feet and the open goal ahead of him. He didn't have time to think. He just hit the ball the way his instincts told him.

There was a clap like thunder as every seat in the stands folded shut and the whole crowd jumped to their feet. Then the roar grew until it seemed to shake the sky above the ground.

"A goal! A goal! Chichico has scored!"

Our books are tested
for children and young people by
children and young people.

Thanks to everyone who consulted on
a manuscript for their time and effort in
helping us to make our books better
for our readers.